Neighborhood Nonsense

By Jill Eggleton

Illustrated by Fraser Williamson

Rigby

Neighborhood Nonsense

Mr. and Mrs. Fitz are occupants of 6 Nite Street. They keep over one hundred hens in their small backyard. Neighbors are complaining!

Mr. and Mrs. Fitz

THE ISSUE IS:

Should Mr. and Mrs. Fitz be allowed to keep hens in the backyard of their Nite Street house?

Suzie Long
Neighbor

Mr. and Mrs. Fitz live in town and have a small backyard. The backyard is not designed for so many animals. In my opinion, Mr. and Mrs. Fitz should not be allowed to keep the hens.

I am a neighbor of the Fitzs. I find the constant clucking of their hens very annoying. There is no escape from it. Sometimes the noise is so loud, I can't even hear the television. I have to wear ear plugs on days when the clucking is unbearable.

The hens drop feathers, too. The feathers blow into the backyard. On windy days, the feathers blow down into the backyards of other people. I am constantly raking up feathers and stuffing them into trash bags. I can't keep my windows open, as I have had feathers floating into my house. Once, I even found a feather in the salad I had made for lunch!

However, the worst problem is the smell. The smell gets into every corner of my house. It is so terrible that visitors have stopped coming over.

I think Mr. and Mrs. Fitz should be more considerate of their neighbors. If they want to have that many hens, they should move to a country area with a suitable backyard.

Suzie Long
Neighbor

Action and Consequence:

ACTION	CONSEQUENCE
the hens drop feathers	the feathers blow down the street
?	?

3

Milly Morris is a resident on Nite Street. She wants to create a kids-only park in a vacant lot on the street.

Milly Morris

4

Should Milly Morris be allowed to turn the **vacant** lot into a kids-only park?

Owen Simmons
Resident

Many of the houses on Nite Street have very small backyards, so the kids play in the street. In my opinion, a 'kids' park' is a sensible idea. Kids on Nite Street often kick balls up and down the pavement. Balls have smashed windows and lights, bounced on roofs, and rolled onto the road in front of cars. This is very dangerous. Kids have been screeching up and down the street on skateboards and bikes, using fences as ramps, and churning up grassy areas.

Old people are too frightened to go out, for fear they will be knocked over. The street is dominated by kids who own scooters, skateboards, and bikes, causing those who don't to stay inside watching television.

At the moment, the empty lot on Nite Street is a home for rats and other vermin. It makes Nite Street look scruffy. It could be turned into a very attractive kids' park with places for skateboarding, biking, and ball games. Having a park on the street would be much safer. Parents would know where their kids are. Kids who watch television most of the time might get outside into the fresh air more. There would always be something for kids to do.

I would like to see the residents of Nite Street volunteer time and make the empty lot into a kids' park. It would be an investment in the future.

Owen Simmons
Resident

Clarify:

What is meant by

. . . It would be an investment in the future?

The Barrets at 11 Nite Street collect lights. They have lights of every description all over their house. Neighbors are complaining!

The Barrets

THE ISSUE IS:
Should the Barrets be asked to remove their lights?

Sam Freno
Neighbor

The Barrets have collected an amazing number of lights and attached them to their house and placed them over trees and shrubs in their garden. They have colored lights, flashing lights, search lights, infrared lights, and laser lights. While other people on Nite Street decorate their homes with lights at the holidays, the Barrets keep their lights on all year. In my opinion, the Barrets should not be asked to remove their lights. The Barrets' house is a bright symbol on Nite Street. Lights are cheerful; they can be a sign of celebration. With the Barrets' house always lit up, the residents on Nite Street can celebrate all year.

Nite Street has become a tourist attraction. People from all over the world come to look at the Barrets' light collection. The lights are so bright that people can stay outdoors long after dark. Neighbors of the Barrets have dinner outside, and can even read books in their backyard. They are saving their own power!

Since the Barrets have had the lights on their house, there have not been many burglaries on Nite Street. It is far too light for burglars. The lights are fascinating for the kids on Nite Street, and an excellent distraction for crying babies who are wakeful during the night.

I think the Barrets should not be asked to remove their lights. The Barrets' house is different, fascinating, and cheerful and makes Nite Street an interesting street to live on.

Sam Freno
Neighbor

Inference:
What inferences can you make about the sort of people the Barrets might be?

Some kids in Nite Street get allowances, others don't.

Kids of Nite Street

Should kids be given allowances?

May Christie
Resident

Some parents give their kids allowances each week. Kids are able to spend this money however they want. In my opinion, kids should not get allowances.

The kids on Nite Street who get an allowance are using it to bribe the kids who don't. I have seen kids with money asking other kids to carry their bags, do their homework, or even borrow their jackets and shoes! The kids without allowances sometimes pretend to be friends with those who do have money. This is encouraging kids to be friends because of what they have, not because of who they are.

The kids with allowances always seem to be eating junk food — chips, fizzy drinks, candy bars. Most kids like junk food and don't realize that too much junk food can be harmful. With money in their pocket, it is hard to control the urge not to buy a candy bar or two every day after school.

If kids receive a weekly allowance from their parents, they could grow up thinking that money comes easily and wonder why they should bother working.

I think allowances should be banned and kids should instead have jobs to do on Nite Street. There are plenty of suitable jobs for kids. They could pick up trash, read books to younger kids or help elderly people. Instead of money, they might receive a voucher that could be spent on a book or a movie.

May Christie
Resident

Question:

Why do you think the kids who don't get an allowance might pretend to be friendly with those kids that do get an allowance?

Jackson is a junk collector; every Saturday he sells junk from the garage at his house.

Jackson Simon

THE ISSUE IS:
Should Jackson be allowed to have a garage sale every Saturday?

Francis Skudder
Neighbor

During the week, Jackson Simon collects junk from the dump and stores it in his garage. On Saturday, people come to buy his junk. In my opinion, Jackson should not be permitted to have a garage sale at his house every Saturday.

Every Saturday morning, the people on Nite Street are woken by cars roaring down the street to Jackson's house. It is not possible for anyone to sleep in. This is very annoying, especially for people who have had to work late the night before.

The street is full of cars and there is nowhere for anyone else to park. Some people are in such a rush to get to Jackson's that they park in front of driveways and owners can't get their cars out.

There are always people hanging around on Nite Street on Saturdays. Sometimes there are arguments about who had the junk first. This is not a good example for the kids on Nite Street. Some people load their trucks up with so much junk, that bits and pieces of junk fall off, littering the street.

I think that Jackson should find a store to rent in town and begin a junk business.

Francis Skudder
Neighbor

Fact or Opinion:

This is not a good example for the kids on Nite Street.

Is this Fact or Opinion?

Fact: A statement that can be proved to be true

Opinion: A view or belief that is not based on fact or knowledge

11

Mrs. Tucker feeds stray cats. Some people in Nite Street are annoyed!

Mrs. Tucker

Should Mrs. Tucker be feeding stray cats?

Albert Hall
Resident

For months now, Mrs. Tucker has been putting food out for stray cats. The cats come in droves down Nite Street, straight to Mrs. Tucker's house. In my opinion, Mrs. Tucker is being kind to unfortunate animals and should continue to feed the cats.

Nite Street has its share of homeless cats. They are thin, straggly, neglected animals who do not know a warm fire, cosy lap, or comfortable chair. There are too many cats for Mrs.

Tucker to take into her home, but by giving them scraps of food, she is helping make their lives a bit better.

People are complaining that a bunch of skinny cats living on Nite Street is giving the street a bad name. But the cats are harmless. Once they have eaten, they disappear again until the next night.

Mrs. Tucker is an old lady. She can't do much to help other people. Giving food to stray cats makes her feel she is still useful and important in some way. She has grown attached to the cats and looks forward to their daily visit. It gives her a purpose to the day.

Mrs. Tucker is showing kindness and generosity. She is a good example to others. I think Mrs. Tucker should be encouraged to feed the stray cats. Other people could help by giving her scraps of leftover food.

Albert Hall
Resident

Character Profile:

Which words would best describe the character of Mrs Tucker?

eccentric?   kind?   selfish?

lonely?   caring?

People on Nite Street mow their lawns at all different times.

A Mower

Should mowing lawns on Nite Street be restricted to a certain time of the day?

Dave Bobbin
Neighbor

People mow their lawns on Nite Street whenever they want to. There are a lot of lawns on Nite Street, and that means lawnmowers can be going all day, every day. In my opinion, lawn mowing should only be done during restricted times.

A lawnmower is very noisy. It is annoying to have a peaceful day shattered by the drone of a lawnmower. People mow their lawns whenever they want, so sometimes the street is never without the sound of a lawnmower. No sooner has one person finished than another one starts.

With lawnmowers whirring away, it is impossible to have a conversation without shouting. Or you could be watching TV when someone decides to mow their lawn. You have to turn up the volume so that you can hear the TV. Sometimes the lawnmower interferes with the TV reception, and makes the picture fuzzy.

I think there should be a law restricting times for lawn mowing. Hours could be between 10 and 12 on Saturday morning. Anyone mowing lawns on Nite Street outside these times should then be fined.

Dave Bobbin
Neighbor

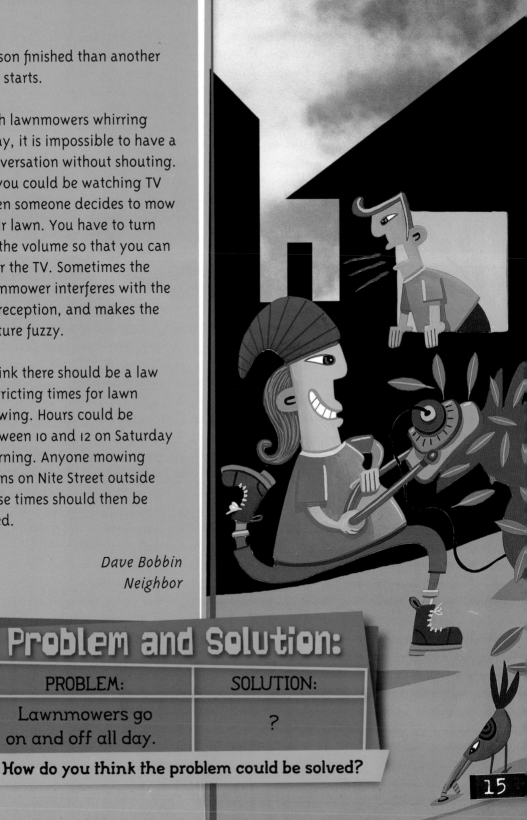

Problem and Solution:

PROBLEM:	SOLUTION:
Lawnmowers go on and off all day.	?

How do you think the problem could be solved?

Mr. Bigelow bought two houses in the middle of Nite Street. He wants to convert one house into a carry-out restaurant.

Mr. Bigelow

BIGELOW'S BIG EAT

THE ISSUE IS:
Should Mr. Bigelow be permitted to open a carry-out restaurant in the middle of Nite Street?

Fran Joseph
Resident

Nite Street is a street that people live in. It has never had stores of any sort. In my opinion, Mr. Bigelow should not be allowed to have a carry-out restaurant. Carry-outs have to be open long hours. This means that people could be coming to Nite Street for carry-out late at night. Cars stopping and starting and people talking and shouting are disturbing for Nite Street residents, who may be trying to sleep.

The smell of food cooking would drift down Nite Street.

People who live on Nite Street would not be able to escape the smell. It could make them feel sick.

The carry-out would have lots of trash, and cans with the smell of food still in them. This would attract flies, mice, rats, and other disease-infested vermin.

A carry-out restaurant in the street could make people lazy about cooking. Instead of cooking meals at home, they would find it much easier to grab something from the carry-out. Kids prefer eating this kind of food. They would see the restaurant and smell the food, and could start pestering their parents for carry-outs every night.

I do not think a carry-out restaurant belongs on Nite Street. Mr. Bigelow could rent out his spare house to people who are having trouble finding a place to live.

Fran Joseph
Resident

Clarify:

What is meant by

. . . *disease-infested vermin?*

17

The Nite Street School is considering having a compulsory uniform. The uniform color is to be entirely lime green.

The Kids

Should Nite Street School have a compulsory lime-green uniform?

Jack Hopper
Resident

The kids who attend the Nite Street School wear whatever they want, and whatever colors they like. In my opinion, a compulsory lime-green uniform would be excellent and very original.

Kids go to school in all sorts of gear. Sometimes they look like they are going to a costume party, and other times as if they belong on a sports team!

Most school uniforms are dull — grey, black, or navy. Dull uniforms could make kids feel dull. Lime green is not dull! Kids would be happy to put on their bright and cheerful lime-green uniform.

No other school has a lime-green uniform. The Nite Street kids would stand out and be noticed. They would feel good about wearing something different and cool. A lime-green uniform would give them pride in their school and a feeling of belonging. Kids would not have to worry about what to wear. Kids would not be bullied or teased if they are wearing something other kids don't think is cool. A whole school at assembly in lime-green uniforms would be a spectacular sight.

I think that the Nite Street School should introduce the lime-green uniform and invite TV and newspaper reporters. The school will become famous and kids from everywhere will be wanting to go there.

Jack Hopper
Resident

Question:

What would your opinion be on having a compulsory lime-green uniform?

Think about the Text

MAKING CONNECTIONS — What connections can you make to the events explored in *Neighborhood Nonsense*?

considering other opinions

reacting to a problem

formulating an opinion

Text-to-Self

being persuasive

debating an issue

showing concern and common sense

Text-to-Text

Talk about other persuasive arguments you have read that have similar features to those in *Neighbourhood Nonsense*. Compare the texts.

Text-to-World

Talk about situations in the world that might connect to elements in the text.

Planning a Persuasive Argument

1 Select an issue you have heard about that is causing you concern.

2 Decide which viewpoints of the issue you agree or disagree with.

3 Make an opening statement in which you identify the issue, and state your own viewpoint strongly.

Mr. and Mrs. Fitz live in town and have a small backyard. The backyard is not designed for so many animals. In my opinion, Mr. and Mrs. Fitz should not be allowed to keep the hens.

Suzie Long
Neighbor

4 Give some reasons or examples that support your point of view.

I think Mr. and Mrs. Fitz should be more considerate of their neighbors. If they want to have that many hens they should move to a country area with a suitable backyard.

A Persuasive Argument usually:

A Is written in the first person

B Uses short paragraphs and sentences

C States the writer's opinion strongly

D Uses examples and facts to support the viewpoint

E Uses emotive words to convey the writer's feelings

F May be serious or humorous or convey sarcasm or anger

G Can conclude with the writer's real or made-up name